This is the back of the book!
Please start the book from the other side...

Native manga readers read manga right to left to keep the manga true to its original vision. To enjoy, turn over and start from the other side and read right to left, top to bottom.

Follow the diagram to see how it's done!

HELLO
MY NAME IS
SHIO

I'm TAMAGO!

If you see the logo below, you'll know that this book is published in its original native format.

NATIVE MANGA
READ RIGHT TO LEFT

An Ancient Evil

From Acclaimed Sci/Fi Horror Writer
HIDEYUKI KIKUCHI

"...this is my vampire masterpiece.
In my personal opinion, this book
transcends Vampire Hunter D."

Rises From Beyond...

Available

DECEMBER 2009

A Novel

YASHAKIDEN
夜叉姫伝
1
the Demon Princess

WRITTEN BY:
HIDEYUKI KIKUCHI

ILLUSTRATED BY:
JUN SUEMI

VOL. 1 ISBN:978-156970-145-4   **$13.95**

DIGITAL MANGA PUBLISHING
dmpbooks.com

● FIRST PUBLISHED IN "MARGARET EXTRA" MAGAZINE, BEGINNING WITH 1990 JUNE ISSUE

N-NO
WAY...!

IT HAPPENED IN SPRING, TWO YEARS AGO...

NOW, FROM THE STUDENT REPRESENTATIVE OF THE INCOMING CLASS, A WORD OF GREETING TO THE CURRENT STUDENTS.

...IN THE LECTURE HALL DURING THE SCHOOL ENTRANCE CEREMONY.

I KNEW THAT, BUT...

I FELL IN LOVE WITH HIM.

I KNOW... HE'S A GENIUS.

FOR SOMEONE LIKE ME, WHO GOT GROUPED INTO THE VERY BOTTOM CLASS BASED ON MY LOUSY SCORES, HE'S OUT OF MY REACH. I KNEW THAT.

AND HE'S... SAYING ALL KINDS OF DIFFICULT WORDS WITHOUT EVEN LOOKING AT THAT PAPER IN HIS HAND — HAS HE GOT HIS SPEECH MEMORIZED?!

OH... OH MY GOSH, NO WAY! HE'S TOTALLY HANDSOME!

WELL... THAT WAS MY DREAM, ANYWAY.

BUT AS LONG AS WE'RE AT THIS SCHOOL, US BEING IN THE SAME CLASS IS JUST... NEVER GOING TO HAPPEN.

WE COULD POSSIBLY —...

IT'D BE GREAT IF WE GOT INTO THE SAME CLASS NEXT YEAR.

THEN I'D DEFINITELY MAKE FRIENDS WITH HIM...AND THEN MAYBE —... JUST MAYBE —

SOMEHOW, I GET THE FEELING HIGH SCHOOL IS GOING TO BE SO MUCH FUN!

9

IF ONLY I'D GIVEN IT SOME THOUGHT, I COULD HAVE SEEN THAT I'D GET REJECTED.

IT'S LIKE YOU ALL SAID — I WAS RECKLESS.

SO, IT'S OKAY. I'LL FORGET HIM.

O-OKAY...

I MEAN, HE WOULDN'T EVEN READ MY LETTER — WHAT KIND OF GUY IS THAT? I OBVIOUSLY HAVE NO TASTE IN MEN.

A HEARTLESS GUY LIKE THAT —...

YEAH... I'LL FORGET HIM.

HEY! SETTLE DOWN! THE BELL RANG AGES AGO!

TOTAL DESTRUCTION

JUST...

MURMUR

MURMUR

JUST OUR HOUSE...

RIGHT?

AND THEY JUST BUILT IT, TOO.

OH, MY!

WOW...

AND NOW, THE 7 O'CLOCK NEWS.

YESTERDAY, THE 16TH, AT 7:10 P.M., THERE WAS AN EARTHQUAKE IN THE CENTRAL KANTO DISTRICT.

TOKYO EXPERIENCED A SMALL TREMOR OF MAGNITUDE 2, WHILE OTHER AREAS FELT A SLIGHT SHAKING OF MAGNITUDE 1.

BECAUSE OF THE QUAKE, THE HOME OF ONE SHIGEO AIHARA-SAN (52) WAS DESTROYED.

AND SHE WAS JUST REJECTED BY IRIE-KUN YESTERDAY... POOR THING!

IT WAS IN THE PAPERS, TOO!

DID YOU SEE THE NEWS?

IT'S HER HOUSE!

IT'S AIHARA-SAN FROM CLASS F.

BAD LUCK COMES IN WAVES.

WHISPER

WHISPER

WHISPER

WHISPER

WHISPER

WHISPER

28

STAFF: Masako Katagai, Yoriko Minato, Shizuko Iijin, ❀ Fusako Kuramochi, ❀ Chiaki Hijiri

AT MY FRIEND'S PLACE, OVER IN THE NEXT TOWN.

SO, WHERE ARE WE GOING TO STAY?

IT'S YOUR FAULT FOR CHEAPING OUT ON THE COST OF MATERIALS, DAD!

B-BE QUIET.

TO THINK THAT THE WOOD IN THE MAIN SUPPORT BEAM WAS RIDDLED WITH TERMITES...

...BUT HE WAS ALWAYS WAY, WAY SMARTER THAN ME.

HE'S BEEN A GOOD BUDDY OF MINE EVER SINCE JUNIOR HIGH...

WOW... HE'S A NICE PERSON.

THEN, JUST RECENTLY, I RAN INTO HIM... AND OUR FRIENDSHIP GREW EVEN DEEPER! HE ALWAYS PROMISED TO VISIT OUR BRAND-NEW HOUSE, BUT AFTER HE HEARD WHAT HAPPENED, HE SAID WE *HAD* TO COME STAY AT HIS PLACE.

"IRI-CHAN"?

A NICKNAME.

I WENT ON TO INDUSTRIAL SCHOOL, BUT IRI-CHAN MADE IT ALL THE WAY UP TO TODAI (TOKYO UNIVERSITY)!

YEAH, IRI-CHAN IS THE BEST!

33

34

40

42

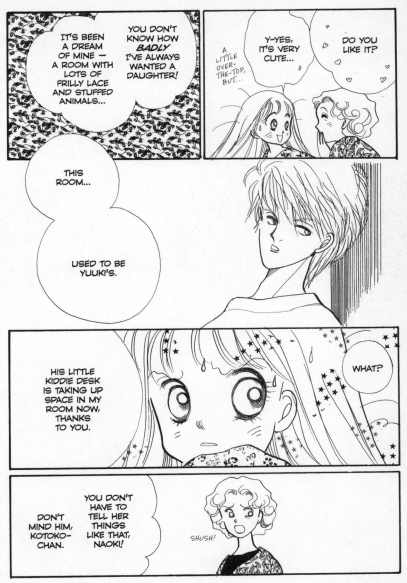

44

OH...

TAP
TAP
TAP

I'LL BE DOWN-STAIRS GETTING DINNER READY.

NAOKI, BE A DEAR AND HELP KOTOKO-CHAN SORT OUT HER THINGS.

OH, THAT'S RIGHT. YOU'VE GOT NO REASON TO RECEIVE ANY HELP FROM ME.

SO, WHAT SHALL I START HELPING YOU WITH?

IT... IT'S ALL RIGHT!

I'LL DO IT MYSELF!

45

I CAN'T.
BELIEVE...

...I'M EATING
BREAKFAST
WITH
IRIE-KUN.

50

51

55

SO ANGRY!

NO WAY, YOU'RE COMING BY TRAIN FROM NOW ON?

OH HEY, KOTOKO!

HE MAKES ME SO ANGRY...

WHAAAT?!

MIDTERMS WILL COVER EVERYTHING UP TO PAGE 56.

3-F

AND SO —

I'VE ALREADY GIVEN UP!

UGH... I AM SO NOT LOOKING FORWARD TO MIDTERMS.

I DON'T THINK I CAN GET AWAY WITH A RED (FAILING) SCORE THIS TIME.

YOU SHOULD HAVE NO PROBLEMS IF YOU WERE PAYING ATTENTION.

WHAT'S THE PROBLEM? IT'S ALL STUFF WE COVERED IN CLASS.

SCHEDULE FOR MIDTERM TESTS

	21	22	23
1	MOD. JAPANESE	PHYSICS	MATH 2
2	ENGLISH β	WORLD HISTORY	CLASSICAL LIT.
3	MATH 1	ENGLISH α	

DING DONG

NO WAAAY

58

ZING!
きっ

ぱリ

I'M SERIOUS!

NOT ONLY IS HE THE TOP STUDENT AT THIS SCHOOL, BUT THE TOP GENIUS IN ALL OF TOKYO!

MAYBE EVEN ALL OF JAPAN!

SOME-THING'S WRONG WITH KOTOKO!

HEY... ARE YOU FEELING OKAY?

KOTOKO'S GONE NUTS~!

IN THE ENTIRE HISTORY OF THIS SCHOOL, NO ONE FROM CLASS F HAS EVER MADE IT INTO THE TOP 100!

KOTOKO! THE PUBLIC ROSTER ONLY SHOWS THE NAMES OF THE TOP 100 SCORES!

DON'T YOU GET IT?

Y-YEAH, WELL...I JUST MEANT THAT'S HOW HARD I'M GONNA STUDY, THAT'S ALL.

ALREADY BACK-PEDALING!

I...I'M GOING TO DO IT!

WELL, I'M GOING TO CHANGE HISTORY!

A-AT THE VERY LEAST, I'M GOING TO GET MY NAME UP ON THE PUBLIC ROSTER!

60

IT'S CALLED "KNOWING YOUR PLACE."

I KNOW THERE'S NO WAY I CAN WIN AGAINST HIM, BUT...

...I'M AT LEAST GOING TO GET MY NAME UP ON THE SAME BOARD AS HIS!

62

63

WHY DON'T YOU TAKE A LITTLE BREAK?

IF I COULD DO THAT —

JUST ASK HIM IF THERE'S ANYTHING YOU DON'T UNDERSTAND, KOTOKO-CHAN.

SUDDENLY, I'VE LOST ALL MY WILL TO STUDY...

WAIT HERE A SECOND, OKAY?

THERE'S SOMETHING INTERESTING I WANT TO SHOW YOU!

OH, OKAY.

-:GIGGLE!:- JUST TAKE A LOOK.

OH...! COULD IT BE THAT THESE ARE NAOKI-KUN'S —

AN OLD PHOTO ALBUM...

HERE!

MEMORIES

WASN'T HE CUTE, THOUGH?

W—

WHAT?!

BUT THIS IS A GIRL...!

SO YOU CAN IMAGINE MY SHOCK WHEN NAOKI WAS BORN.

THAT'S WHY I ONLY BOUGHT GIRL'S CLOTHES.

I WAS EVEN CONVINCED I WAS GOING TO GIVE BIRTH TO ONE.

YOU SEE, I REALLY, *REALLY* WANTED A GIRL.

I WONDER IF IT'S WHAT TURNED HIM INTO SUCH A COLD FISH?

NAOKI RESENTS ME FOR IT TO THIS DAY.

BEET!

MAY, 1975 WITH DAD

I JUST DECIDED TO DRESS HIM IN THEM!

BUT I DIDN'T WANT TO LET THE CLOTHES GO TO WASTE, SO...

...RIGHT UP UNTIL THE TIME HE FINALLY STARTED BECOMING AWARE OF THINGS LIKE GENDER, AND SAID NO.

66

68

70

71

THAT'S NOT EVEN POSSIBLE!

HUH? THEY'RE FIGHTING!

F-FORGET IT!

KOTOKO... DID SHE CONFESS HER LOVE AGAIN... AND GET REJECTED AGAIN?

AHHHH!

FLAP

OKAY, THEN I'LL JUST MAKE COPIES OF THIS AND STREW IT AROUND THE WHOLE SCHOOL...

...
...
...

STARTING TODAY, I'LL TUTOR YOU IN THE EVENINGS FOR A WEEK.

FINE.

SQUEAL

BUT I GUARANTEE NOTHING.

77

W-WHOSE FAULT DO YOU THINK IT IS?!

IT WAS NOTHING.

BEHOLD THE POWER OF KOTOKO-CHAN!

THAT'S WONDERFUL! NAOKI, STUDYING FOR A TEST~

GOOD LUCK, KOTOKO-CHAN~

...
...

WELL, LET'S GO GET STARTED.

Y-YES!

YOU DON'T NEED HELP.

B-BIG BROTHER, HELP ME STUDY, TOO!

THEN WE'LL GO WITH THAT.

NOW THAT WE'RE ALONE, I'M SO NERVOUS...

BA-BUMP

BA-BUMP

BA-BUMP

I HAD A CRUSH ON HIM FOR TWO WHOLE YEARS, AFTER ALL...

WHAT'S YOUR WEAKEST SUBJECT?

SO, WHAT DO YOU WANT TO START WITH?

NERVOUS~

キンチョ〜

M-MATH, I GUESS.

82

...HE'S JUST A NORMAL, CUTE-LOOKING GUY...

WHEN HE'S LIKE THIS...

KNOCK KNOCK

I'VE BROUGHT YOUR SNACK —

OH...!

THE CAMERA, THE CAMERA!

WHOOSH!

O-OH MY!

...I USED TO LOVE AND ADMIRE...

IT'S THE IRIE-KUN...

SO TODAY'S THE DAY, KOTOKO-CHAN!

86

ENGLISH

...AS THE ONES IRIE-KUN THOUGHT UP!

THIS ONE, TOO!

OH — THIS PROBLEM ...!

MODERN JAPANESE

MATH

THEY'RE EXACTLY THE SAME...

AND THUS, THE LONG WEEK IS...

DING DONG DING

...FINISHED!

WHAT? DON'T SOUND SO COCKY.

YOU'LL FEEL FOOLISH LATER!

I... I THINK I DID OKAY!

WHEW—

SO, HOW DID YOU DO, KOTOKO?

PARTY TIME~!

90

91

93

YOU'RE RIGHT, BOSS.

THIS BEARS SOME LOOKING INTO.

THAT'S A GOOD QUES- TION, BOSS.

PLUS...HOW DID KOTOKO HAVE TIME TO STUDY SO MUCH WHEN SHE'S BEING TREATED LIKE A SLAVE AT HER TEMPORARY LODGINGS?

REALLY THINKS IT'S TRUE!

WOMEN SURE TALK A LONG TIME...

UGH...

THEY SURE DO, BOSS.

OKAY.

SAME HERE, SATOMI! HEY, WANNA STOP FOR SOME ICE CREAM ON THE WAY?

THE TRIP HOME IS SO FUN NOW THAT YOU TAKE THE SAME TRAIN AS I DO, KOTOKO! I'M SO HAPPY!

98

AS ALWAYS, IRIE-KUN COMPLETELY IGNORES ME.

DARN HIM!

...I'VE GOTTEN PRETTY GOOD AT DODGING THE PERVS.

BUT RECENTLY...

GLARE

BUT I GUESS I ONLY HAVE TO PUT UP WITH IT UNTIL OUR NEW HOUSE IS BUILT...

OH, THAT'S RIGHT! I'D FORGOTTEN ALL ABOUT IT.

WHAT'S THIS? A GOOD LUCK CHARM?

I GOT IT FOR THE MIDTERMS WE JUST HAD.

GOOD LUCK CHARM FOR KOTOKO-CHAN ON HER TEST DAY ♡

HUH? YOU DROPPED SOMETHING, KOTOKO.

MORNING!

WAFT!

* _SUGAWARANO MICHIZANE_ WAS A REGARDED POET AND POLITICIAN OF THE HEIAN PERIOD, AND AFTER HIS DEATH WAS DEIFIED AS THE GOD OF SCHOLARSHIP

HUSH, SILLY!

WELL, WHOEVER'S PIC IS IN THERE BRINGS MORE GOOD LUCK THAN _SUGAWARANO MICHIZANE!_

HMM... SHE SAID TO OPEN IT AFTER THE TEST RESULTS WERE ANNOUNCED.

SURE WAS EFFECTIVE, THOUGH.

IT FEELS PRETTY LIGHT FOR A GOOD LUCK CHARM.

IT'S LOUDMOUTH KIN-CHAN AGAIN...

KOTOKO!

A-ARE YOU LIVING...

AT NAOKI IRIE'S HOUSE RIGHT NOW?!

THERE'S SOMETHING I WANT TO ASK YOU...

STAGGER...

STAGGER...

W-WHAT HAPPENED TO YOU, KIN-CHAN? YOU LOOK SICK... AND PALE.

105

106

108

114

115

118

121

122

WE WON'T GET CAUGHT! BESIDES, DIDN'T YOU GUYS SAY YOU'RE CURIOUS ABOUT HOW THOSE TWO LIVE TOGETHER, TOO?

WHAT IF WE GET CAUGHT?

I'M NOT SURE ABOUT PEEPING INTO IRIE-KUN'S HOUSE, KIN-CHAN.

IRIE-KUN SEEMS SCARY...

BE CAREFUL...

HNNGH!

THAT IRIE...JUST LET ME SEE HIM MAKE ONE MOVE ON KOTOKO, AND I'LL —

KNUCKLE SANDWICH TIME!

HERE IT IS!

WE'RE WASTING A PERFECTLY GOOD SUNDAY...

WELL... SURE, BUT NOT CURIOUS LIKE YOU, KIN-CHAN!

WHAT'S THIS FUNNY-LOOKING DISH OVER HERE?

HEY — YOU'RE RIGHT!

WOW, IT LOOKS DELICIOUS!

THERE! EVERYONE DIG IN!

S-SO TIRED...

G-GULP-

HAHAHA! THAT'S BECAUSE IT WAS SO GOOD!

YOUR EYES ARE TEARING UP, DAD.

NOW EVERYONE ELSE HAVE SOME!

OH... OHHH — THAT WAS SOOOO GOOD!

BLEAH!

Y-YUCKY!

AT THIS RATE, I FEAR NO MAN WILL EVER WANT TO MARRY HER.

SHE'S ALWAYS BEEN A TERRIBLE COOK. SHE DOESN'T TAKE AFTER ME AT ALL!

I WISH I WERE SO DEAD RIGHT NOW...

N-NO, NO — IT'S DELICIOUS!

...I THOUGHT SO.

SLUMP...

IT'S OKAY, IRI-CHAN... YOU DON'T HAVE TO BE SO POLITE.

128

BUT IF SHE COMES HERE, YOU CAN JUST LIVE WITH US, TOO!

IF KOTOKO-CHAN GOES OFF TO GET MARRIED, YOU'LL BE LEFT ALL ALONE — RIGHT, AIHARA-SAN?

あ STUNNED... け

WE COULD EXPAND THIS HOUSE TO ACCOMMODATE A THREE-GENERATION FAMILY, AND ALL LIVE HAPPILY TOGETHER!

IT'D BE SUCH A WASTE OF MONEY, ANYWAYS...

WHY DON'T YOU JUST GO AHEAD AND HALT THE RECON-STRUCTION OF YOUR HOUSE?

HOW ABOUT IT, AI-CHAN?

HMM... YES, I COULD DO THAT...

OHHH, THAT'S A WONDERFUL IDEA — I'M ALL FOR IT!

I'D BECOME RELATIVES WITH AI-CHAN!

D-DAD!

HMM...WELL, COMPARED TO MARRYING KOTOKO OFF TO A COMPLETE STRANGER, IT'S —...

131

137

NYAAH-

147

...TO MY OBSERVATION DIARY!

SUMMER RESEARCH HOMEWORK
KOTOKO OBSERVATION DIARY

THIS IS A GREAT START...

CLANK

JUST LIKE A LITTLE RICH BOY!

HOW ELEGANT?

AWW, OUT FOR A GAME OF TENNIS TODAY, GENIUS?

YO.

I DON'T ENVY YOU, THAT'S FOR SURE.

HELLO THERE, BOY GENIUS.

WELL, THERE'S NO TELLING WHEN A GENIUS MIGHT SUDDENLY TURN INTO A WOLF, YOU KNOW?

HMPH!

PLAYING CHAPERONE EVERY MORNING OF THE REVIEW CLASSES FOR A WEEK?

W-WHAT DID YOU SAY?!

TROMP TROMP
スタ スタ

YES, YOU'RE RIGHT. I GUESS SHE HAD BETTER BE CAREFUL.

TREMBLE
わな
わな
TREMBLE

S-SORRY TO KEEP YOU WAITING!

→WHEEZE
→HUFF
→GASP
→HUFF

WEREN'T YOU SUPPOSED TO BE "THE IRIE OF CLASS F"?

HUH? WHY'S KIN-CHAN WITH YOU?

HELLO!

MORNING, KOTOKO.

3-F

REVIEW CLASSES

ZEEK-
ZEEK-
ZEEK-

150

155

156

158

BUT MOTHER, THE FROSTING LOOKS GROSS...

NOW, LET'S CUT THE CAKE! GO AND GET BIG BROTHER, YUUKI.

SQUIRT SQUIRT

SPLAT...

BY THE WAY, DAD —

G-GEE, I HAVE NO IDEA. I HAVEN'T LOOKED AT IT LATELY. I'LL GO CHECK IT OUT SOON.

I SEE...

SHOULDN'T IT BE FINISHED BY NOW?

WHAT'S THE STATUS OF OUR HOUSE?

HUH?

JUMP!

161

STAFF: AKI ISHIKAWA, MASAKO KATAGAI, SHIZUKO IIJIN + CHIAKI HIJIRI   THANK YOU VERY MUCH ♥

163

WHAT? RIGHT NOW?

GOOD IDEA! YOU NEED TO GET OUT OF THAT HORRIBLE IRIE HOUSE AS SOON AS POSSIBLE!

DAD WON'T TELL ME ANYTHING ABOUT HOW IT'S GOING!

YEAH, I THINK I'LL JUST GO SEE FOR MYSELF HOW FAR ALONG THE CON-STRUCTION ON OUR HOUSE IS.

WE AGREE ON SOME-THING!

I SECOND THAT.

YEAH, JUST AROUND THIS CORNER.

WOW, I HAVEN'T BEEN HERE IN AGES!

IT'S AROUND HERE, RIGHT?

UGH, I BET IT'S ANOTHER TRADITIONAL JAPANESE-LOOKING —...

167

168

SILENCE ─── しーん

Y-YES?!

HEY.

WELL... WHAT? WHAT IS IT?!

UGH... CAN I GET THROUGH THE NEXT TWO DAYS?

YOU'RE IN CHARGE OF DINNER TONIGHT.

→HUFF←

→HUFF←

OH...

OKAY.

-:GIGGLE!:- THAT PART ABOUT GRANDMA BEING ILL WAS A LIE.

WHAT REASONS?

THERE ARE A *LOT* OF REASONS BEHIND THIS TRIP.

QUIT POUTING, YUUKI.

IT WAS A PLOY I DEVISED TO GET YOUR BROTHER AND KOTOKO-CHAN ALONE TOGETHER!

WHAT?!

I HAD THE LADY AT THE RICE SHOP FAKE THAT PHONE CALL FOR ME. OH, I'M SUCH A GOOD ACTRESS!

SHE WAS SO IMPRESSED!

AND SINCE THE DADS ARE OUT ON THEIR LITTLE TRIP, I WANTED US THIRD WHEELS TO BE AWAY, TOO.

THOSE TWO ARE SO ROMANTICALLY-IMPAIRED! I THOUGHT THIS WAS A GOOD CHANCE TO MAKE THEM GET TO KNOW EACH OTHER BETTER.

I WANNA GO BACK HOME!

174

177

RUMMAGE
IS IT IN THIS DRAWER -?
OR MAYBE IN HIS BAG...
RUMMAGE
RUMMAGE
I'VE GOTTA FIND IRIE-KUN'S NOTES... IRIE-KUN'S —
O-OOPS, I FORGOT I'VE GOT NO TIME TO WASTE!
RUSTLE
MATH III
SUMMER REVIEW TEXT
THE COMPLETE ANSWERS... THE HOLY GRAIL...!
F-FOUND IT — !
...AND GET TO COPYING IMMEDIATELY!
WELL, NOW I'LL JUST SKEDADDLE...
HUH?
3-A NO.1 NAOKI IRIE

186

I'LL SPREAD IT THROUGHOUT THE ENTIRE SCHOOL!

I'M GOING TO TELL EVERYONE YOU ATTACKED ME!

GO AHEAD.

YOU FORGOT THIS.

...I CONCEDE.

HUH?

THERE ARE ENOUGH RUMORS FLYING AROUND AS IT IS. WHAT'S ONE MORE?

EVERYONE'S ALREADY LETTING THEIR IMAGINATIONS RUN WILD.

MATH III

HEY.

URK...

189

* THE ISONO FAMILY FROM THE CARTOON "SAZAE-SAN," IS A NOSTALGIC MODEL OF THE CLOSE-KNIT JAPANESE FAMILY

IT'S THE SECOND SEMESTER, SO IT'S TIME TO START THINKING SERIOUSLY ABOUT YOUR COURSE OF ADVANCEMENT.

ALL RIGHT —

EVERYONE GOT A COPY OF THE PRINTOUT?

3-F

ADVANCEMENT QUESTIONNAIRE

FURTHER EDUCATION 2 EMPLOYMENT

PLEASE WRITE DOWN WHERE YOU HOPE TO GO NEXT FROM HERE.

195

200

202

さーて練習するかーっ

DON'T BE STUPID! DO YOU WANT TO LOSE TO CLASS A IN THE CO-ED RELAY?

I HAVE AN ERRAND TO RUN.

KOTOKO, SATOMI, NEMOTO - ! HURRY UP!

NO OTHER CLASS IS TRAINING.

WHAT A PAIN!

UGH... KIN-CHAN'S SO INTO IT...

UH, WHY THE HECK ARE WE DISCUSSING ORDER IF IT'S ALREADY DECIDED?

DUMMY! YOU HAVE TO HAND ME THE BATON, KOTOKO! THEREFORE, YOU'RE THIRD!

W-WHY DO I HAVE TO?

OH! THEN I WANT TO BE THE FIRST GIRL TO GO!

I, OF COURSE, WILL BE THE ANCHOR.

FIRST, LET'S DECIDE THE RUNNING ORDER FOR THE FOUR OF US.

SCRATCH

SCRATCH

4321

203

204

30 MINUTES LATER...

206

207

209

SO THIS ROOM WILL BE NAOKI AND KOTOKO-CHAN'S BEDROOM —

HMM, ALL RIGHT. THEN IS IT OKAY IF WE TURN THIS ONE INTO A KARAOKE ROOM, MOTHER?

AND THIS ROOM WILL BE RESERVED FOR WHEN THEY HAVE A BABY.

SO, SHALL I TELL THE BUILDERS THAT CONSTRUCTION ON MY HOUSE IS OFFICIALLY CANCELED?

OKAY, WE'LL MAKE IT *THIS* ROOM.

NO, USE THE BASEMENT.

OH NO, THAT'S DIRECTLY ABOVE THE BABY'S ROOM!

...WE'LL PUT THIS PLAN INTO ACTION RIGHT AWAY, AND THEN —

NEXT YEAR, WHEN THE TWO OF THEM HAVE GRADUATED...

WHAT PLAN?

* VICTORY! TODAY'S THE DAY – CLASS 1F

* WE'RE NUMBER ONE! 2-F

THE GAUDY BANNERS... THEY'RE ALL CLASS F, FROM EVERY GRADE LEVEL...

* TONAMI HIGH SCHOOL ATHLETICS FESTIVAL

THE COFFEE IRIE-KUN MADE FOR ME...

...SOMEHOW TASTED UNUSUALLY BITTER.

AND THE OVER-THE-TOP ENTHUSIASM IN THESE BANNERS JUST MAKES IT THAT MUCH SADDER...

IT'S LIKE WE'VE BET OUR ENTIRE FUTURES ON TODAY...

INCLUDING CLASS A, NONE OF THEM LOOK TO TAKE THIS SERIOUSLY AT ALL.

I MEAN, LOOK AT ALL THE OTHER CLASSES WITH THEIR SIMPLE SIGNS.

3 — A

3 — B GO

YOU TWO ARE OFFICIALLY A COUPLE, NOT ONLY IN THE EYES OF THE ENTIRE CAMPUS, BUT YOUR PARENTS, TOO...

BUT IT MEANS NOTHING IF IRIE-KUN REFUSES TO ACKNOWLEDGE IT.

URK...

HEEEY, KOTOKO~!

MRS. IRIE WAS REALLY INTO IT, SO...

BUT THE IRIE FAMILY'S BANNER IS THE MOST EXTRAVAGANT OF THEM ALL.

KOTOKO~ CHAAAN~!

215

216

217

218

221

222

235

236

240

YOU LOOK SO TIRED!

OH, MY! WHAT'S WRONG, KOTOKO-CHAN?

OH... OKAY...

IT'S NOTHING...

기기...
WOBBLE...

기기...
WOBBLE...

기기...
WOBBLE...

SHE DOESN'T HAVE A CHOICE.

B-BUT—

YOU SHOULDN'T PUSH YOURSELF TOO HARD OVER STUDIES, DEAR.

GOOD-NESS!

I'M STUDYING FOR THE FINALS THAT START NEXT WEEK...

YUP, YUP!

WHO DID YOU TAKE AFTER TO TURN OUT SO DENSE?

KOTOKO, THAT'S PATHETIC!

IT'S A LIFE-DETERMINING MOMENT FOR SOMEONE IN CLASS F.

THIS TEST WILL DETERMINE WHETHER SHE CAN ADVANCE TO COLLEGE.

YOU.

241

242

THEY'RE ALL UGLY.

YŪKI!!

I MUST GO AND MAKE YOU ALL SOME TEA!

WE'VE NEVER HAD SO MANY GIRLS IN THIS HOUSE BEFORE!

THANK YOU—

THIS IS *SOME* TASTE IN INTERIOR DÉCOR YOU HAVE, KOTOKO!

FRILL

FRILL

WOW—

FRILL

FRILL

YIKES! BEYOND THIS WALL SITS THE GENIUS!... CAN YOU HEAR ANYTHING?

NEXT DOOR.

HEY, SO WHERE'S IRIE-KUN'S ROOM?

MRS. IRIE LOVES THE GIRLY-GIRL STUFF.

247

248

250

H-HE IS A GENIUSSSS -!

I- INCREDIBLE!

EVERY STEP OF EVERY PROBLEM IS WRITTEN IN A CLEAR AND CONCISE MANNER!

WHAT'S GOING ON?

3-F

MUMBLE

BUT WHAT ABOUT OTHER SUBJECTS BESIDES PHYSICS?

AND THIS PART IS GOING TO BE ON THE PHYSICS TEST, TOO!

THANK GOD — NOW I'M SAVED IN PHYSICS!

HURRAY -!

THREE CHEERS FOR IRIE-SAMA!

AFTER ALL, IT'S JAPAN'S NUMBER-ONE GENIUS, IRIE-KUN, WHO SOLVED THEM!

CERTAIN-LY.

AHEM! えっへん

NOW THIS IS EASY TO UNDER-STAND!

OF COURSE IT'S BECAUSE IT WAS US WHO ASKED THAT HE DID THIS!

OOH, LET US COPY IT -

255

PLEASE, IRIE-KUN - PLEASE -

...
...
...

I'M
HOME —

NAOKI —
IN THE LIVING
ROOM — !

→SQUEAL←

HUH?
WHAT?

→SQUEAL←

HE'S
PLAYING
TEACHER!

DEAR!
DEAR —
YOU WON'T
BELIEVE IT!

W-WHOA!
WHAT'S WITH
THIS MOUNTAIN
OF SHOES?!

どや どや
MOUND   MOUND

IF I WANT TO STUDY, I CAN DO IT ON MY OWN — I DON'T NEED SOMEBODY TO TEACH ME.

W-*WHAT?!* W-WHY WOULD SOMEONE LIKE *YOU* NOT GO TO COLLEGE?!

WELL, WHAT IS IT THAT YOU WANT TO *BE?*

ーっっ...URK...!

YOU'LL NEED A DEGREE FOR WHATEVER CAREER YOU WANT TO GO INTO... AND THERE'RE CLUBS TO JOIN, AND PARTIES TO GO TO...

BUT THAT'S NOT THE ONLY REASON TO GO!

YOU HAVE TO USE THEM FOR THE BETTERMENT OF JAPAN!

BUT YOU'RE DIFFERENT, IRIE-KUN. YOU CAN'T KEEP YOUR BRILLIANT BRAINS ALL TO YOURSELF.

...
...

FOR THE MOMENT, I GUESS I WANT TO BE ABLE TO HELP DAD OUT AT THE RESTAU-RANT...

I... HADN'T REALLY THOUGHT ABOUT IT, BUT...

SO I'D HAVE TO LEARN HOW TO COOK A BIT.

SEMESTER FINAL EXAMS
(LAST DAY)
FIRST PERIOD - MODERN JAPANESE 9:00 ~
SECOND PERIOD - PHYSICS 10:00 ~

OKAY —
LAST FIVE
MINUTES!

MAKE
SURE YOU
INCLUDED
YOUR
NAMES ON
THE TEST.

DING
DONG
キーン
コーン

PENCILS
DOWN.
PASS YOUR
PAPERS UP
TO THE
FRONT.

IT'S
OVER - !

HOW'D
YOU DO,
KOTOKO?

I WAS
ABLE TO
FILL IN
MOST
OF IT!

YAAY - !

JUST
NOW...

THANKS
AGAIN!

...I
FEEL
AS IF
I GOT
JUST A
LITTLE
PEEK
INTO
IRIE-
KUN'S
HEART.

270

STAFF: AKIKO ISHIKAWA, MASAKO KATAGAI, SHIZUKO IIJIN, KANAMI SUDO   THANK YOU VERY MUCH!

WE'LL BE ON SCHOOL BREAK STARTING TOMORROW, TOO.

...SINCE I'M ALWAYS IN HIS DEBT.

I DON'T HAVE A CLUE ABOUT WHAT IRIE-KUN WANTS...

BUT —

WHAT TO GET HIM?

LOW-FREQUENCY PULSE MASSAGER

COMRO

COMRO

15,000

HMM...

WHAT SHOULD I GET HIM?

IT'S ALREADY TOO LATE TO MAKE A SWEATER...

HE PROBABLY WOULDN'T WEAR IT ANYWAY.

OH, AND I CAN'T KNIT!

I DOUBT HE'D LIKE ANYTHING AN AVERAGE MALE WOULD APPRECIATE...

ALL RIGHT — AS SOON AS IRIE-KUN OPENS THE DOOR, EVERYONE —

HERE HE IS!

ONE, TWO...

GET READY, GET READY!

WELL, ENJOY YOUR-SELVES.

KOTOKO, YOU DIDN'T SPILL THE BEANS, DID YOU?

H-HUH? HE'S NOT ACTING SURPRISED.

TURN

I DIDN'T?

POP—!

POP—!

IF YOU WANTED TO SURPRISE ME, YOU SHOULD HAVE DONE SOMETHING TO HIDE THE MOUNTAIN OF SHOES IN THE DOORWAY.

...
...
...

W-WAIT, IRIE-KUN!

MERRY CHRISTMAS, IRIE-KUN!

A MASSAGER —?! HOW UNROMANTIC! NICE TASTE, KOTOKO!

WHAT IS THAT, BIG BROTHER?

...
...

H-HUH? REALLY? YOU THINK?

A LOW-FREQUENCY PULSE MASSAGER.

DOOOM: がーん

IT'S A GIFT FOR *OLD PEOPLE*.

OH...UH... W-WAITRESSING...

SO *THAT'S* WHY YOU WERE ALWAYS COMING HOME SO LATE! WHAT KIND OF JOB?

...

UH, NO — NOT REALLY... I JUST TOOK A LITTLE PART-TIME JOB AND —...

BUT THIS WAS EXPENSIVE, WASN'T IT, KOTOKO-CHAN?

281

THIS IS FOR YOU, KOTOKO-CHAN!

DIG IN, EVERY-ONE!

WOW, WHAT A PRETTY PICTURE FRAME!

IT'S FROM ME AND FATHER.

W-WHAT? FOR ME?

HOW ABOUT A PHOTO OF YOU HUGGING KOTOKO-CHAN...

NAOKI, AS YOUR PRESENT TO KOTOKO-CHAN...

OF COURSE NOT.

AND NAOKI, DO YOU HAVE ANYTHING FOR —

WHA-... WHAAAAT ?!

...TO GO INSIDE THE PICTURE FRAME?

THAT'S WHAT I THOUGHT. SO I HAVE AN IDEA!

282

284

EVERYONE EXCEPT HIM, THAT IS.

GLANCE...

RIGHT NOW, EVERY HIGH SCHOOL SENIOR IS CRAMMING LIKE THERE'S NO TOMORROW...

IT'S UNBELIEVABLE!

HE'S JUST SITTING THERE, WATCHING NEW YEAR'S PROGRAMMING ON TV.

BUT...

* HYAKUNIN-ISSHU IS A CARD GAME WITH A SPECIAL DECK CONTAINING ARTWORK THAT CORRESPONDS TO LINES OF POETRY. THE CARDS ARE SPREAD OUT, AND ONE PERSON READS ALOUD A CARD WITH A LINE OF POETRY, WHILE THE PLAYERS HUNT FOR THE CARD THAT CORRESPONDS TO THAT PARTICULAR LINE. IT'S A GAME THAT IS TRADITIONALLY PLAYED AT NEW YEAR'S.

A GENIUS HAS GOT TO WALK A GENIUS'S PATH.

COME ON – LET'S START WITH HYAKUNIN-ISSHU!

SO *HE IS* GOING TO TAKE THE COLLEGE EXAMS. I THOUGHT SO.

HERE.

PAF

"KORE-YAKO -.."

HMMMM

YOU *COULD* LOSE TO SAVE FATHER A LITTLE BIT OF FACE, NAOKI.

I CAN'T BELIEVE I LOST TO MY OWN SON...

URGH... WE'RE NO MATCH.

YOU'RE ALL TOO WEAK.

WOW, YOU WON *AGAIN!*

YOU'RE AMAZING, BIG BROTHER!

293

EEEEE -!
NOOO -!

FLUSH.

WELL,
I GUESS THAT
SETTLES IT —
I WON'T BE
GOING TO T-DAI.

OH...

THAT
WAS NO
CONTEST.

STUPID
KOTOKO!

HAHAHA!

I'M SO
SORRY -!

I'M SO
SORRY,
MR. IRIE -!

...

I-I'M
SORRY,
MR. IRIE -!

THIS IS
ABOUT THE
ONLY THING
I CAN DO
FOR HIM...

WHEW...
THIS
GOOD LUCK
CHARM FOR
THE EXAM
IS ALMOST
DONE.

I-I'M
SURE
HE WAS
JUST
JOKING...

I'M
WORRIED...

NOT THAT
IRIE-KUN
NEEDS IT,
BUT...

お守り

* GOOD LUCK

IRIE-KUN
WILL GO
TO T-DAI...
WON'T
HE?

* FUGU-KICHI

GEE, AI-CHAN —

THANKS SO MUCH FOR TODAY!

AH, WELL, MY KOTOKO'S ALWAYS CAUSING YOU TROUBLE, SO IT'S THE LEAST I COULD DO.

THANK YOU, MR. AIHARA.

THIS PLACE ISN'T MUCH, BUT I'D LIKE HIM TO FILL UP FOR ENERGY!

THINK NOTHING OF IT! AFTER ALL, TOMORROW IS NAOKI-KUN'S EXAM DAY.

HEY, KOTOKO! GET THE BEER!

OH! WHY DON'T YOU TAKE HIM UP ON THAT, NAOKI?

MOTHER LOVES TATSUO UMEMIYA'S PORTRAYAL OF A CHEF, YOU KNOW!

WELL, I HAD ALWAYS PLANNED TO HAVE KOTOKO'S EVENTUAL HUSBAND TAKE OVER AND EXPAND IT, BUT...

THIS IS A NICE LITTLE PLACE YOU'VE GOT, AI-CHAN!

...

WELL, LET'S HAVE A TOAST —

OH, THANK YOU!

HERE YOU ARE, SIR!

* TATSUO UMEMIYA IS A JAPANESE ACTOR.

かんぱ KANPAI-! い

GOOD LUCK TO YOU TOMORROW, NAOKI!

299

* KOTOKO'S "ITADAKI-MAMMOTH!" IS A SILLY PUN OF THE JAPANESE PHRASE, "ITADAKI-MASU," WHICH MEANS, "I WILL HAVE SOME." THIS SILLY "MAMMOTH" PUN PHRASE (AND OTHERS) USED TO BE A TRADEMARK OF A JAPANESE ACTRESS NAMED NORIKO SAKAI, WHO ALSO WENT BY THE NICKNAME "NORI-P."

300

302

304

COME NOW, NAOKI — YOU NEED A HEAD-START. I'M WORRIED THE TRAINS MAY BE LATE BECAUSE OF THE SNOW.

YEAH.

FORGET IT.

IT'S MY OWN FAULT FOR TRUSTING YOU.

TH-THROW IT UP, *QUICK!*

O-OH NO!

...
...

I HAVE A BAD FEELING ABOUT THIS...

I'LL GO TO THE STATION WITH YOU!

B-BETTER NOT *TRIP* AND *FALL!*

ZWOOSH

ZWOOSH

W-WOW —

O-OH — UM, IRIE-KUN...

WELL, LATER.

OH NOOO I SLIPPED !

PLONK

← EXAM STUDENT

* IN JAPAN, THE WORDS "SLIP," "TRIP," OR "FALL" ARE TABOO AROUND STUDENTS FACING EXAMS, SINCE THE WORDS ARE SYNONYMOUS WITH FAILING, AND CONSIDERED A BAD OMEN.

...IT'S A GOOD LUCK CHARM FOR YOUR EXAM!

TH-THIS MAY NOT BE MUCH USE, BUT...

WOULD YOU TAKE IT WITH YOU?

I PRAYED REALLY HARD WHILE I WAS MAKING IT.

TICKET GATE

HURRY UP—! HEEEY, IRIE—!

I'M SURE IT'LL BRING YOU LOTS OF LUCK!

I'LL JUST ATTACH IT TO YOUR BAG, OKAY?

CUT IT OUT!

H-HEY—

COMING.

SO PUSHY...

WHAAAT?

WHEN DID I EVER SAY THAT? I'VE *NEVER* THOUGHT THAT, *EVER!*

I THOUGHT YOU DIDN'T REALLY WANT ME TO GO TO T-DAI?

HAS NO MEMORY!

...
...
...

308

310

COLLEGE ENTRANCE
TEST CENTER
EXAMS
THIS WAY ➡

HUFF
ハァ

HUFF
ハァ

ゴホ
KOFF

ゴホ
KOFF

TWO STATIONS AWAY...GOD, I HAVEN'T RUN THIS MUCH *IN* YEARS.

ゴホ
KOFF

ゲホン
KOFF

HOW FAR DID YOU END UP GOING?

I'M SO GLAD! YOU MADE IT JUST UNDER THE WIRE!

OH — IRIE!

SLIP
ポロ

LET ME GET IT OFF — I WANT TO GET RID OF IT AS SOON AS POSSIBLE.

OH — IT'S STILL ON THERE.

WHAT HAPPENED TO THE GOOD LUCK CHARM?

BAD LUCK CHARM IS MORE LIKE IT!!

おやり

OH!

I'VE GOT A BIT OF A COLD.

YOUR FACE LOOKS FLUSHED, IRIE. YOU MIGHT HAVE A FEVER.

REALLY?! OH NO!

IRIE? THE ONE WITH A 200 I.Q.?

THAT'S HIM...

* GOOD LUCK

312

IT'S ALREADY GONE.

I TAKE IT BACK, MAN — GET RID OF THAT CHARM AS SOON AS POSSIBLE!

OF COURSE I'M *NOT* OKAY.

Y-YOU OKAY?

...
...

...
...

UH... IRIE-KUN, IS IT?

パラ FLAP

パラ FLAP

AH...

YES.

PRESENT YOUR EXAM TICKET.

WHA-...

EXAM TICKET
No 1208

NAME: IRIE, NAOKI

GO FOR IT!

IT'S NOT THAT I DON'T UNDERSTAND IT, BUT PLEASE ERASE THESE KINDS OF THINGS NEXT TIME.

HUH?

315

316

321

BUT THIS IS IRIE-KUN — HE *NEVER* MESSES UP. I'M SURE HE DID OKAY!

SCARY...

OH MY, HE REALLY *IS* EDGY.

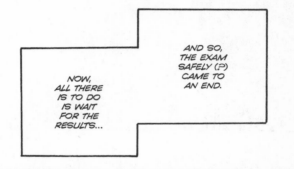

AND SO, THE EXAM SAFELY (?) CAME TO AN END.

NOW, ALL THERE IS TO DO IS WAIT FOR THE RESULTS...

IT-...

IT'S HERE!

IT'S HERE, NAOKI!

IN REAL LIFE, RESULTS ARE NOT MAILED OUT LIKE THIS...

REALLY?! THE TOP?! OH, I DO REMEMBER HEARING THAT THE TOP SCORE IN THE NATION WAS 996...

B-BY THE WAY, I JUST HEARD CONFIDENTIALLY FROM THE TEACHER ABOUT IRIE GETTING THE TOP SCORE...?

YEAH, I DID OKAY.

WOW, I'M HAPPY FOR YOU!

HOW WERE YOUR RESULTS, WATANABE-KUN?

I WAS JUST ON MY WAY OVER TO IRIE'S.

HUH? "THAT SITUATION"...?

A SCORE OF 996...IN THAT SITUATION...

A-AMAZING...

+ NAOMI WATANABE   THANK YOU VERY, VERY MUCH! (♥)

LUCKY CHARM?

I'D NEVER SEEN HIM LOOKING LIKE THAT BEFORE.

GOD, IT WAS TRAGIC.

EVEN IF IT WAS ALL THE FAULT OF THAT HOMEMADE LUCKY CHARM —

328